POST CARD

First published in 2005 by
MACMILLAN
Children's Books
A division of Macmillan Publishers Limited

20 New Wharf Road, London N1 9RR
Basingstoke and Oxford
Associated companies throughout the world
www.panmacmillan.com

ISBN 1 405 05082 9

1 3 5 7 9 8 6 4 2

THIS SPACE MAY BE USED FOR
PRINTED OR WRITTEN MATTER

Text and illustrations copyright © Emily Gravett 2005
Moral rights asserted. Printed in China

A CIP catalogue record for this book is available from the British Library.

For
Oleander Grrrabbit
(because I love you)
and the pottery pals
(because I promised)
X X X

NEW IN AT YOUR LIBRARY!

WOLVES

Emily Grrrabbit

Burrow WOLVES and many other rip-roaring tails at your local library NOW!

MACMILLAN CHILDREN'S BOOKS

Rabbit went to the library.
He chose a book about . . .

WOLVES

WEST BUCKS
PUBLIC BURROWING
LIBRARY
☎ 0123 43210

Telephone 0123   43210

West Bucks Public Burrowing Library

Please return or renew on or before the last date stamped
A fine may be charged if items are returned late

03/07/1991		
12/06/1992	26/04/1997	
02/10/1992		09/03/2002
07/12/1993	07/10/1997	
29/05/1994		08/05/2002
17/06/1995	14/02/1998	10/05/2003
		17/03/2004
20/06/1995	28/07/1998	
		04/04/2004
20/11/1996		12/02/2005
14/02/1997	22/09/2000	09/08/2005
		24/09/2005

GREY WOLVES live in packs of
between two and ten animals.

They can survive almost anywhere:
from the Arctic Circle . . .

. . . to the outskirts of towns and villages.

In some areas wolves have retreated
to places where fewer people live,
such as forests and woodland.

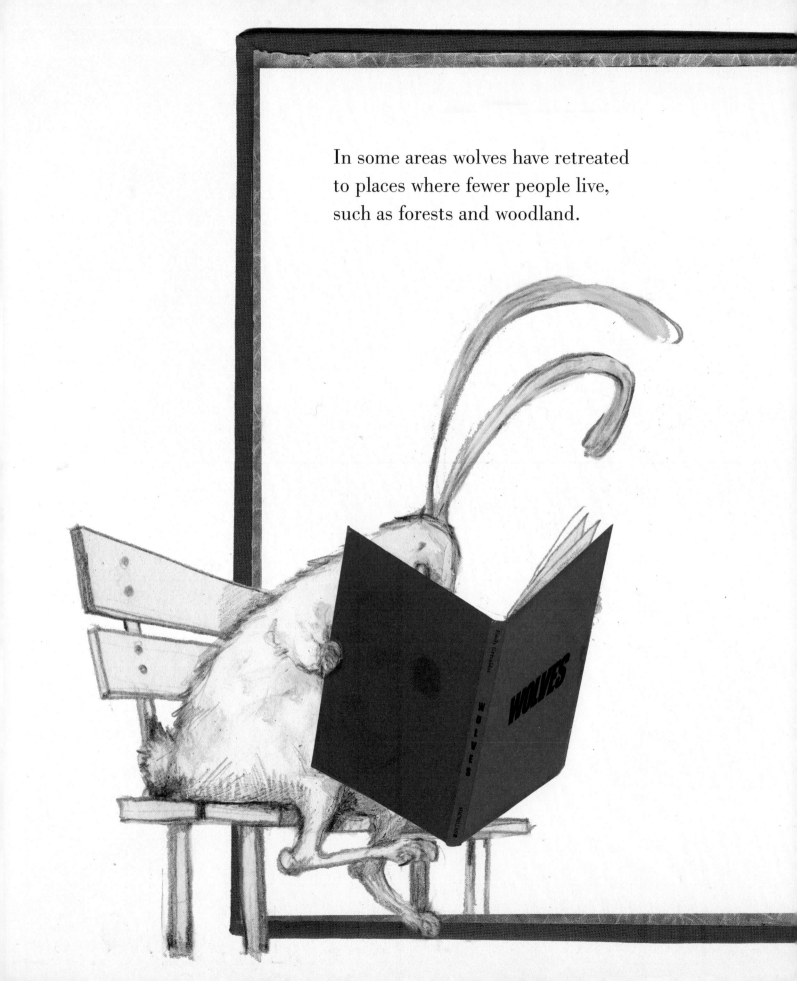

They have sharp claws...

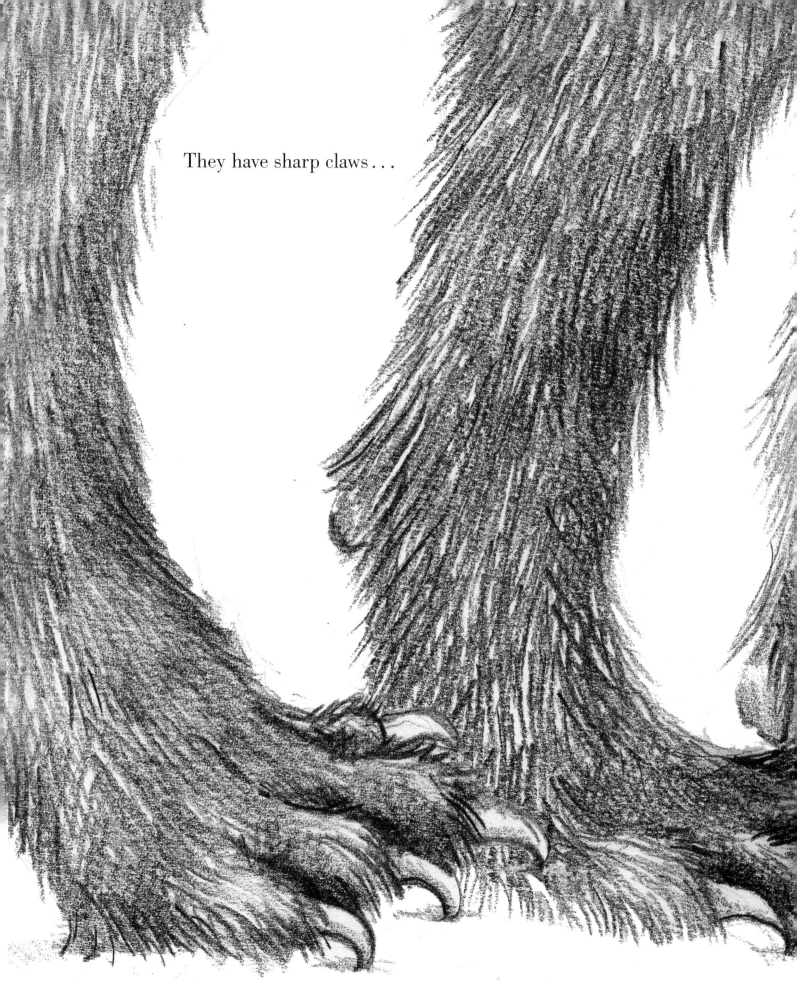

. . . bushy tails . . .

. . . and dense fur, which harbours fleas and ticks.

An adult wolf has 42 teeth.
Its jaws are twice as powerful
as those of a large dog.

Wolves eat mainly meat. They hunt large prey such as deer, bison and moose.

They also enjoy smaller mammals, like beavers, voles and . . .

. . . rabbits.

The author would like to point out
that no rabbits were eaten during
the making of this book.
It is a work of fiction.
And so, for more sensitive readers,
here is an alternative ending.

Luckily this wolf was a vegetarian, so they shared a jam sandwich, became the best of friends, and lived happily ever after.

If undelivered please return to
West Bucks Public Burrowing Library
36 Warren Wood
Nibbleswick

Burrow more books

鼠竹筷 Burrowed Wok

Carrotense
Take Away

43 RABBIT RUN · THE HUTCH
DITCHLING ROAD · SALAD PATCHAM
TELEPHONE ORDERS WELCOME

TELEPHONE 260497

DELIVERY SERVICE AVAILABLE
7 EVENINGS A WEEK

From: 5.30pm – 11.00pm

Within 3 Miles £1.00. 4-5 Miles £1.50

FREE Lawn Crackers
on orders over £10

FREE Morning Dew
on orders over £30

· OPENING HOURS ·

Monday - Thursday	5pm - 11.30pm
Friday - Saturday	5pm - 12 Midnight
Sunday	5pm - 11.00pm

Angora Organics
GARDENING CATALOGUE
Every seed you need for the perfect patch.

G. RABBIT
LANE'S END BURROW
THE LONG FIELD
NIBBLESWICK

RABBIT MAIL
POSTAGE PAID
HQ 6733
GREAT BURROW